The GINGERBREAD MAN

LOOSE in the SCHOOL

Laura Murray · illustrated by Mike Lowery

SCHOLASTIC INC.
New York Toronto London Auckland
Sydney Mexico City New Delhi Hong Kong

To Kyle, caitlyn, and Bridget—
my three smart cookies.
And to chris, my co-baker.
—L. M.

This book is dedicated to Allister,
an amazingly awesome daughter.
And thank you to Katrin
for all of her help.
—M. L.

ISBN 978-0-545-48593-7

Text copyright © 2011 by Laura Murray. Illustrations copyright © 2011 by Mike Lowery. All rights reserved. Published by Scholastic Inc., 557 Broadway, New York, NY 10012, by arrangement with G. P. Putnam's Sons, a division of Penguin Young Readers Group, a member of Penguin Group (USA) Inc. SCHOLASTIC and associated logos are trademarks and/or registered trademarks of Scholastic Inc.

26 25 24 23   15 16 17/0

Printed in the U.S.A.   40

First Scholastic printing, September 2012

Design by Ryan Thomann
Text set in Bokka and Dr. Eric, with a bit of hand-lettering
The illustrations were rendered with pencil, traditional screen printing, and digital color.

I began in a bowl.
I was not yet myself—

just a list of ingredients
pulled from a shelf,

SUGAR

GINGER

SALT

chosen by children who **measured** and **mixed**
my smooth, spicy batter while sneaking quick **licks** . . .

Yummy!

A sprinkle of ginger, some cinnamon too,

molasses, soft butter, and eggs as my **glue**.

Then in their classroom, the children began to **roll** me and **mold** me to look like a **man**.

FINALLY, I thought,

I'M A GINGERBREAD MAN!

I picked up my **toe**

and I hopped down the **hall,**

then into a room
that was tidy and small.

NURSE

The **nurse** came right over.
She squatted down **low.**

I **pointed** and showed her
my broken-off **toe.**

She fixed up my toe with a small dab of glue,
then reached for a **bandage** and stuck that on too.

With **spectacular** speed,
I slid to the floor

and bounded right in
through a large wooden **door.**

I **leapt**
for a table,

but landed **inside**
a brown paper bag
with its top
open wide.

I tried to climb out, but I spied two big **eyes.**

They **peered** in the bag with a look of surprise.

"YOUR CLASS PASSED THE ART ROOM JUST MINUTES AGO."

"YOU MIGHT ASK THE PRINCIPAL. MAYBE SHE'LL KNOW."

I leapt from the table. I waved, and then said,

THANKS FOR NOT TAKING A BITE OF MY HEAD.

I'LL SKIP AND I'LL SKIP,
AS FAST AS I CAN.
I CAN CATCH THEM! I'M THEIR
GINGERBREAD
MAN!

I passed through an **office,**

slipped under a **door,**

and discovered a **room** I had yet to **explore.**

And there on the wall was a drawing of me!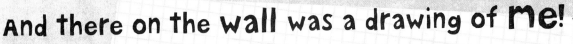

The poster said:

MISSING

FROM ROOM 23.

IF FOUND, PLEASE RETURN HIM AS SOON AS YOU CAN. WE THINK HE IS LOST, HE'S OUR GINGERBREAD MAN.